PRESENTED BY

Dallis Joiner

1st Grade 1999-2000

So, which book to read?

Leonardo DaVintchi | Africa and Russia

Magazine | Archeology | The Lion and The Lamb | Fairy Tales | Bobby | Gerald Ford

Alexandros

WESTMINSTER SCHOOLS   SMYTHE GAMBRELL LIBRARY

VOLCANOES

DANIEL ROGERS

**RAINTREE
STECK-VAUGHN**
PUBLISHERS
A Steck-Vaughn Company

Austin, Texas

Published by Raintree Steck-Vaughn Publishers,
an imprint of Steck-Vaughn Company

Library of Congress Cataloging-in-Publication Data
Rogers, Daniel.
Volcanoes / Daniel Rogers.
     p.   cm.—(Geography starts here)
     Includes bibliographical references and index.
     Summary: Explains how volcanoes are formed, how and why
they erupt, how they can be predicted, and the effects they
can have on people and the environment.
     ISBN 0-8172-5547-8
     1. Volcanoes—Juvenile literature.
     [1. Volcanoes.]
     I. Title. II. Series.
     QE521.3.R644 1999
     551.21—dc21   98-28894

Printed in Italy. Bound in the United States.
1 2 3 4 5 6 7 8 9 0 03 02 01 00 99

Picture Acknowledgments
Pages 1: Image Bank/Richard Ustinich. 5: Bruce Coleman/Werner Stoy.
7: Bruce Coleman/Gerald Cubitt. 8, 9: Photri Inc. 10: Zefa. 12: Getty Images/Paul Kenward. 13: Bruce Coleman/Orion Service
and Trading Co Inc. 15: Bruce Coleman/Fritz Prenzel. 17: Oxford Scientific Films/Breck P Kent/Earth Scenes. 18: Getty
Images/Hideo Kurihara. 19: Photri Inc. 20: Geoscience Features. 21: Rex Features/Pedro Ugarte/Sipa. 22: Rex
Features/Carraro. 23: Photri Inc. 24: Oxford Scientific Films/Richard Packwood. 25: Geoscience Features/Dr. B. Booth. 26:
Photri Inc. 28: Oxford Scientific Films/Colin Monteath. 29: Rex Features/Yves Breton/Sipa. 31: Photri Inc. Cover: Zefa.
Illustrations: Peter Bull.

The title page photo shows the Arenal volcano in Costa Rica.

CONTENTS

A MOUNTAIN OF FIRE

A volcano is a hole or crack in the surface of the earth. Out of this hole comes a fiery substance called magma. Magma is made up of rocks that are so hot they have melted.

Magma comes from deep inside the earth. When it pushes up through a hole and flows onto the surface it is called lava. As the lava cools down it becomes solid rock. Gradually the rock builds up to form a mountain.

A diagram showing the layers of the earth. We live on the thin, surface layer called the crust.

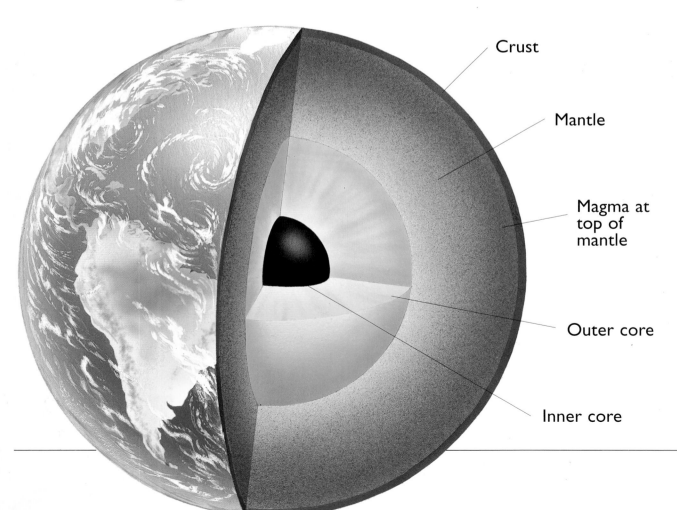

Crust

Mantle

Magma at top of mantle

Outer core

Inner core

Fountains of lava
pour out of Kilauea
in Hawaii.

THE WORLD'S VOLCANOES

Volcanoes are not found everywhere in the world. They occur mostly around the edges of the Pacific Ocean, in a huge band called the Ring of Fire.

There are also groups of volcanoes in East Africa, Iceland, southern Italy, and the Caribbean. There are even some in the frozen continent of Antarctica.

The earth's crust is broken into huge pieces called plates. Most volcanoes are near the edges of plates.

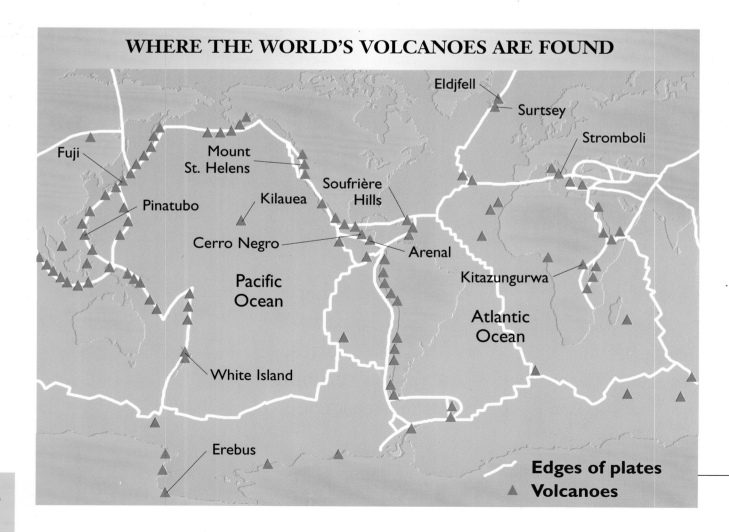

WHERE THE WORLD'S VOLCANOES ARE FOUND

Eldjfell

Surtsey

Stromboli

Fuji

Mount St. Helens

Soufrière Hills

Kilauea

Pinatubo

Cerro Negro

Arenal

Kitazungurwa

Pacific Ocean

Atlantic Ocean

White Island

Erebus

Edges of plates
▲ **Volcanoes**

Once there were volcanoes in many other places, too. Millions of years ago, in parts of Great Britain, France, and North America, volcanoes poured red-hot lava over the land surface. Now, only the rocks they made are left behind.

These volcanoes in Java, Indonesia, are part of the Ring of Fire.

Steam and ash burst from an underwater volcano at the bottom of the Atlantic Ocean.

Volcanoes Under the Sea

There are probably more volcanoes under the world's oceans than there are on land. Usually, we can't see underwater volcanoes because the oceans are so deep. But sometimes a volcano grows until it appears above the surface of the ocean.

The island of Surtsey first appeared off Iceland in 1963. It was made by an underwater volcano.

Some islands in the Atlantic, Pacific, and Indian oceans are actually volcanoes.

WHEN A VOLCANO ERUPTS

When magma breaks through the earth's crust, this is called an eruption. Volcanic eruptions are some of the most powerful forces on Earth. Sometimes a volcano erupts in a huge explosion that can be heard thousands of miles away.

When lava pours from a volcano, it may flow toward towns and villages. The people who live there have to run for their lives.

Lava flows like a river from a volcano in Hawaii.

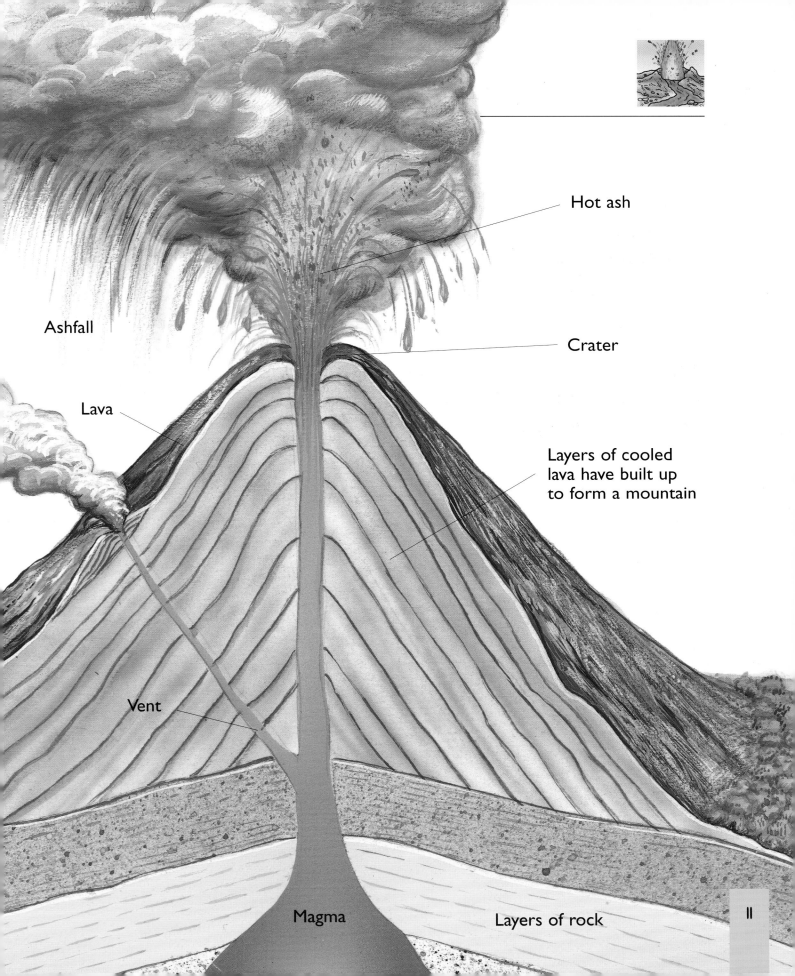

Hot ash

Ashfall

Crater

Lava

Layers of cooled
lava have built up
to form a mountain

Vent

Magma

Layers of rock

Why Volcanoes Erupt

Most volcanoes don't erupt all the time. Although magma is always pushing up toward the surface, it isn't usually strong enough to break through. But eventually the pressure becomes too much, and the magma bursts through weak spots in the crust.

Volcanoes that have not erupted for a long time are called dormant.

White Island Volcano in New Zealand is an active volcano. This means it could erupt at any time.

DISASTER REPORT

Find out as much as you can about the Soufrière Hills volcano that erupted on the Caribbean island of Montserrat in 1997.

Imagine you are a journalist and write a news report describing the eruption. You could draw pictures to illustrate your report.

Fuji, in Japan, is an extinct volcano. This means it has not erupted for hundreds of years.

Volcanic Eruptions

Some eruptions are like explosions. Others are more gentle. If the magma is thin and runny, the gas inside it can escape easily and the magma flows gently from the volcano.

But gas can't escape so easily from thick, sticky magma. As it tries to get out, the pressure builds up until it bursts out and explodes. Bits of magma are blasted into the air.

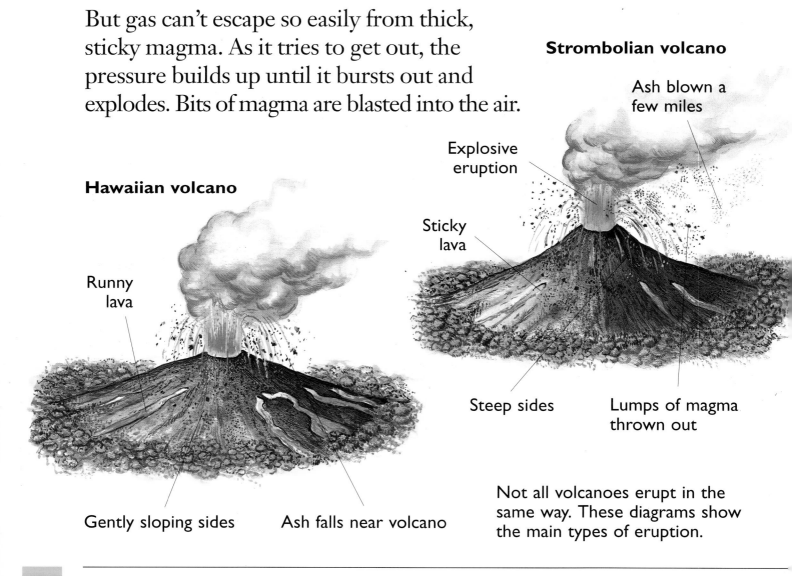

Strombolian volcano

Ash blown a few miles

Explosive eruption

Sticky lava

Steep sides

Lumps of magma thrown out

Hawaiian volcano

Runny lava

Gently sloping sides

Ash falls near volcano

Not all volcanoes erupt in the same way. These diagrams show the main types of eruption.

Stromboli is a volcano in southern Italy. It has given its name to a type of eruption.

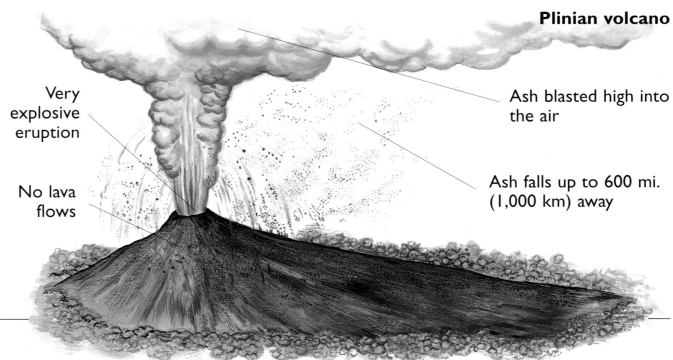

Plinian volcano

Very explosive eruption

No lava flows

Ash blasted high into the air

Ash falls up to 600 mi. (1,000 km) away

After an Eruption

When a volcano has erupted, the area around it may suffer very strong winds and heavy rain. The rainwater then mixes with the ash that has poured from the volcano. This mixture becomes thick mud.

Mud on the sides of the volcano may slide downhill as a mudflow. Mudflows contain thousands of tons of mud and travel very fast. They destroy everything in their path.

The town of Armero, Colombia, was buried by a mudflow in 1985.

When Mount St. Helens, in Washington, erupted in 1980, a huge flow of mud, rocks, and ice destroyed all these trees.

Hot water and steam shoot from a geyser in Rotorua, New Zealand.

Geysers and Mud Pools

In volcanic areas, magma under the ground heats up water that is in the rocks. In some places, the heated water and steam may come to the surface gently in hot springs. In others they may spurt up from the ground as a geyser.

Hot springs sometimes produce large pools of mud at the surface. Hot water and steam bubble up through the mud.

The bubbles of steam make a "plop" sound as they burst in a mud pool.

PEOPLE AND VOLCANOES

Volcanoes can cause terrible damage. Lava flowing over the ground can cover buildings and crops and set them on fire.

The ash that is blown out of a volcano is even more destructive. Huge amounts of ash may fall to the ground like a heavy, gray snowfall. The ash can be so thick that fields, houses, and whole towns are buried under it.

This house is being buried by lava from Eldjfell Volcano in Iceland.

Thick clouds of ash pour from Cerro Negro Volcano in Nicaragua. The ash makes it difficult for people to breathe.

Rescue workers help a survivor after a mudflow in Armero, Colombia.

Imagine your home is on the slopes of a volcano. With your friends, act out what you would do if the volcano erupted. If you had to leave your home and you could take only one thing with you, what would you choose?

Fifty-seven people were killed when Mount St. Helens erupted in 1980.

Volcanic Killers

Volcanoes can bring death as well as destruction. Most people are killed by falling ash, mudflows, and ash flows. An ash flow is a red-hot cloud of volcanic dust that hurtles downhill at more than 60 mph (100 km/h).

In 1991, Pinatubo in the Philippines erupted. More than 700 people were killed by mudflows, ash flows, and by diseases caused by the poisonous ash.

VOLCANOES AND THE ENVIRONMENT

Ash that is blown into the air in an eruption can affect the world's weather for months afterward. The ash blocks out some of the sun's rays, making the temperature colder.

Poisonous gases from volcanoes can cause acid rain. When the gases mix with water in the air, they make acid. The acid then falls to the ground as rain. Acid rain can kill trees and poison lakes and rivers.

Ash from Kitazungurwa Volcano has killed these trees in Zaire.

Volcanic ash and dust in the air can make beautiful sunsets.

Useful Volcanoes

Volcanoes are not always bad. Soil that is made from volcanic lava contains minerals that help plants grow. This soil is very good for farming. Many crops are grown on the slopes of volcanoes.

Rice is grown in the rich volcanic soil of Bali, Indonesia.

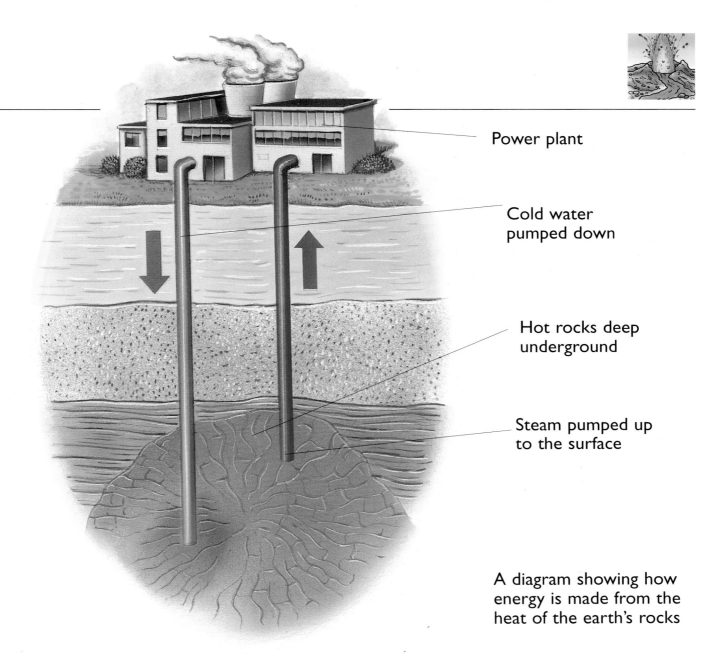

Power plant

Cold water
pumped down

Hot rocks deep
underground

Steam pumped up
to the surface

A diagram showing how
energy is made from the
heat of the earth's rocks

Heat from volcanoes is called geothermal
energy. It can be used to make electricity.
Cold water is pumped down to the hot rocks
deep under the earth's surface. The rocks
heat the water and turn it to steam. The
steam is then piped to a power plant on
the surface.

PREDICTING ERUPTIONS

Scientists can sometimes figure out when a volcano is going to erupt. Special equipment can show them where magma is rising to the surface. The gases coming from a volcano also give clues to what is happening underground.

A scientist going to study the crater of Erebus in Antarctica

When a volcano does erupt, scientists usually know where lava, mudflows, and ash flows are likely to go. But there is not much that can be done to stop them. If people live near a volcano, they have to be ready to leave quickly when it erupts.

Sometimes people try to keep lava from damaging towns and farmland by building a wall of earth and rock in its path.

VOLCANO FACTS AND FIGURES

The world's loudest eruption
When Krakatoa (in Indonesia) erupted in 1883, the massive explosion was heard on the island of Rodrigues, which is more than 2,900 mi. (4,776 km) away.

The worst volcanic killers
The most deadly eruption in history was Tambora, Indonesia, in 1815. It is thought that 92,000 people were killed by huge ashfalls and by starvation. Many people starved because the ashfalls buried the fields and destroyed all the crops.

About 36,000 people died following the eruption of Krakatoa in 1883.

In 1902, the whole town of St. Pierre, on the Caribbean island of Martinique, was destroyed by an ash flow. Only one person survived from a population of 28,000.

When Nevado del Ruiz, in Colombia, South America, erupted in 1985 it set off massive mudflows. The mudflows gushed down the mountain at 56 mph (90 km/h) and buried the town of Armero. About 22,000 people died.

The longest lava flows
The longest ever known was the Roza Flow in North America, which happened about 15 million years ago. It stretched for 186 mi. (300 km) and covered an area of more than 15,440 sq. mi. (40,000 sq. km).

The longest since records began was a flow from Laki, in Iceland, which was about 43 mi. (70 km) long.

The most active volcano
Kilauea in Hawaii has been erupting continuously since 1983.

The tallest geyser
The tallest active geyser is Steamboat Geyser in Yellowstone National Park. It shoots water and steam up to a height of 377 ft. (115 m) above the ground.

The Waimangu Geyser in New Zealand used to reach a height of more than 1,500 ft. (460 m), but it has not erupted since 1904.

Further Reading

Christian, Spencer and Felix, Antonia. *Shake, Rattle, and Roll: The World's Most Amazing Volcanoes, Earthquakes, and Other Forces* (Spencer Christian's World of Wonders). New York: John Wiley and Sons, 1997.

Field, Nancy and Machlis, Sally. *Discovering Volcanoes.* Middleton, WI: Dog-Eared Productions, 1996.

Levy, Matthys. *Earthquake Games: Earthquakes and Volcanoes Explained by Games and Experiments.* New York: Margaret McElderry Books, 1997.

Nelson, Sharlene P. and Ted Nelson. *Mount St. Helens National Volcanic Monument* (True Books—National Parks). Danbury, CT: Children's Press, 1997.

Simon, Seymour. *Volcanoes.* New York: Mulberry Books, 1995.

Stidworthy, John. *Earthquakes and Volcanoes* (Changing World). San Diego: Thunder Bay Press, 1996.

GLOSSARY

Active A volcano that is currently erupting or likely to erupt.

Ash Small piece of magma, less than 2 millimeters across, that is thrown out from a volcano.

Ashfall Small pieces of magma that are blasted out of a volcano and then fall back to Earth.

Ash flow Particles of volcanic ash from an eruption, which are blown down the sides of a volcano at great speeds by hot gases.

Crater The bowl-shaped mouth of a volcano. Craters are caused by eruptions.

Crust The earth's surface layer.

Dormant A volcano that has not erupted for many years.

Eruption When magma, gases, and ash are forced out of a weak spot in the earth's surface.

Extinct A volcano that has not erupted for thousands of years.

Geyser A spring that shoots jets of hot water and steam into the air.

Lava Liquid magma that erupts from a volcano and flows over the earth's surface. Lava eventually cools to become solid rock.

Magma Hot, melted rock that is found beneath the earth's surface.

Mantle The layer of rock beneath the earth's crust.

Minerals The natural substances from which the earth's rocks are made.

Mudflow A mixture of hot, volcanic ash and water that flows down the side of a volcano.

Pressure When something is pressing against something else.

Devil's Tower in Wyoming is all that remains of an ancient volcano.

INDEX